Catching Him

Sporting Pride #2
Charity Parkerson

Punk & Sissy Publications

Copyright

—Warning: This book is intended for readers over the age of 18. Some of my books contain allusions to past abuse and trauma.

CHARITY PARKERSON

Editor: BZ Hercules & Consultants

Photographer: Paul Henry Serres

Contents

Introduction

THERE WAS A TIME when Eric would stay a secret. Those days are gone. Oakley has no intention of hiding him. That's not better.

Eric gave up everything to be with a professional athlete. He put his entire life on hold for his ex's career while the man he loved kept him hidden from the world. Now he has nothing to show for those years but a broken heart and a bucketful of rage. Now there's this new guy whose life is every bit as public. Eric won't make the same mistake twice. Unfortunately, being the secret isn't the only way to end up feeling like the fool.

Oakley spent years in the spotlight, leaving behind an amazing baseball record. He still finds ways to stay relevant. It's possible he's addicted to the attention. Meeting Eric gives him that same rush. The guy doesn't want to want him, and Oakley can't stop chasing him. Winning is in his blood. But the thrill he feels with Eric might not be the hunt. It may actually be his fall.

Catching Him is the second book in Charity Parkerson's Sporting Pride series. These are sports-related romance, following men who find love while navigating high-profile careers. These are best enjoyed when read in order.

Chapter One

SIGNING BASEBALL CARDS NEVER got old. Oakley didn't think he was a narcissist. It was baseball. Being retired changed nothing. There wasn't a day that went by where Oakley didn't thank the universe for allowing him to live his childhood dream. The odds of having the success he had achieved were slim. People were definitely more likely to get struck by lightning. He never forgot that or lost his love for the sport. Every time he thought about how far he had come, he was humbled by life.

Still, by the time his scheduled time ended, Oakley's fingers ached. His back cramped. These baseball conventions kept his face out there, but they were exhausting, especially with his body being abused for years. By the end of the weekend, his face hurt from keeping a smile plastered on it. His throat hurt from talking to fans and speaking on panels. He was still grateful for every second, but he was also tired.

The hotel attached to the convention center was huge and pricey. Everything looked fancy, yet somehow also outdated. He thought about stopping by the bar before heading to his room. Fear of running into more fans stopped him. He felt extra exhausted tonight. Instead, he popped inside the small store next to the front desk and grabbed a drink and snacks before hitting the elevator. Thankfully, he managed to make the ride in silence. As he opened the app on his phone to unlock his room, the phone rang. He didn't recognize the number. Oakley's tired-sounding sigh echoed down the empty hallway. He stumbled over nothing, losing his balance before righting himself. "Fuck." A growl rose in his throat. He let himself inside the room before answering.

"Hello?"

"May I speak with Oakley Wilkes?"

"This is he."

The man's voice on the other end brightened. "Oh, good. Sorry for the late call. This is Baylor Keates. I'm Rocky and Jakk's wedding planner. With the wedding so close, I'm nailing down the final numbers. When you RSVP'd, you didn't mark if you intend to bring a plus one."

Yeah. Oakley had done that. It was complicated. He cleared his throat. "Uh.

Yeah. Sorry. Here's the thing. I haven't had time to talk to Rocky." He also didn't know how to start the conversation they needed to have. "My possible plus one might not be welcome to come to the wedding, so I didn't want to assume anything. If you give me a few days, I can let you know."

A long pause followed by a loud sigh met his rambling. "Don't take this the wrong way, but nobody gives a damn about your plus one." Oakley's eyebrows shot up, but Baylor didn't stop there. "This is the grooms' day. They probably won't even notice if their own families are there, let alone your date. I'm trying to do my damn job and people like you—who make it all about them—make my job hard as hell. All I need to know is if you're bringing a goddamn plus one and if you want fish or chicken."

An uncomfortable chuckle escaped Oakley. The attitude caught him off guard. "Okay.

Damn, sassy. Put me down for a plus one and let it be in your head if the happy couple comes unglued at the sight of my date."

"Thank you." The chipper note to Baylor's voice had Oakley shaking his head. "That's all I needed."

"All right."

"Have a good night."

For a moment, Oakley stood there blinking at nothing, with the phone still pressed to his ear after Baylor disconnected the call. He shook his head again. Oakley couldn't say the guy didn't get shit done. If Oakley ever married, he might have to look into hiring him. Fuck. He had said he would bring a date. There was only person he cared to ask. Unfortunately, Oakley hadn't exaggerated. There was a very real chance Rocky and Jakk would flip their shit. Oakley didn't want to ruin their big day. Then again, Baylor was the expert and probably right. They likely wouldn't even notice Oakley, much less his date. This wedding would be huge. A famous football star marrying a well-known sports agent was a big deal. The crowd at this shindig would be enormous. No wonder Baylor sounded a bit stressed. Oakley couldn't imagine the job he undertook. No one would care who he brought, which was a good thing, since it was Jakk's ex.

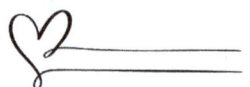

It was hard as hell to go from sharing a huge home with his other half to being stuck in a tiny bedroom at his aunt's place. Not only that, but Eric had a shitty job, zero money, and no hope after giving up everything for a relationship that failed spectacularly. He had failed. Truthfully, there was money in his savings. His ex, Jakk, had set him up an account out of guilt. Eric couldn't bring himself to touch it. He didn't know if it was his guilt or anger. Pride. Jakk didn't know Eric didn't use the money, so the entire situation was dumb. But Eric would know if he touched that money, and it felt a hell of a lot like letting Jakk win. Jakk had only set up that account because he had asked Eric to give up his education, life, and home to follow him for his career. Then he had brutally dumped Eric. Eric had lost track of who was at fault. They both were to an extent. None of that mattered anymore. They were done. Jakk was set to marry soon. Eric was nothing now. He had to let it go.

Eric tried focusing on the way his feet hurt. Not only did he walk everywhere in downtown New York now, but he stood all day for his job. He had been lucky his aunt knew someone who knew someone, allowing him to land a cashier position at a huge company known for paying more than the standard for the area. Still, he was a cashier for a department store. He wasn't moving from his aunt's place. This was forever. That thought alone was enough to make him want to slit his wrists. Eric stared at the bedroom ceiling and tried not to think. He was over Jakk. Anger would do that to a person. He wasn't over the destruction of his life because he had no choice but to keep living it. But Jakk, yeah. He could go fuck himself. His phone rang. Eric checked the face. A slight smile touched his lips at the sight of Oakley's name. Now Oakley was an entirely different story. Eric just hadn't figured out what yet.

"Hello?"

"Hey. How was work?"

Eric switched the phone to speaker and set the device on his chest. He went back to staring at the ceiling. "It was fine. How was the convention?"

"Same as always. I just got an interesting phone call from Rocky's wedding planner."

Eric rolled his eyes. He appreciated Oakley not saying Jakk's name, but he still didn't want to hear about their wedding. "Okay."

"He got pretty upset with me for not specifying if I intend to bring a plus one. So, want to go to a wedding with me?"

Everything inside Eric recoiled at the idea. "No."

Oakley laughed, despite the disgust in Eric's voice. "Come on. There'll be hundreds of people there. They won't even notice us.

We'd get free food and alcohol. You'd get a free trip to Minnesota."

Eric's nose was still curled. "There're so many things I want to say right now, but I'll stick with the civil ones. Not only can I not afford to miss work, I also can't afford a fancy outfit. Even if I could do those things, I would never spend money to go watch my ex marry someone else. Not that I'm jealous," Eric added since he didn't want to look bitter and pathetic, even though he was those things.

"Please?" Oakley broke out the pleading voice on him. "I don't want to go with anyone else. What if I cover your missed wages and buy you whatever you want to wear? Please don't make me go to a wedding alone. That's just... the worst," he finally said, as if no words would do.

In spite of himself, Eric realized he was smiling. "I don't want another man financing me. That's already destroyed my life once."

"You shouldn't look it that way. This is your friend, bribing you to save him. We can get drunk and make fun of their decorations."

Eric couldn't stop smiling. He knew Oakley didn't mean it. Rocky was his friend. In fact, that was how they met. Oakley had accused Eric of stalking Rocky. All because they had been in the same bar at the same time. Unfortunately, that accusation had been how Eric learned Jakk was in love with someone else. But once Oakley realized he was wrong, he had transformed into this really amazing guy. Eric liked being around him. He wished Oakley wasn't also a professional athlete. Retired or not, athletes were cold. They wanted to look manly. They couldn't be gay. Apparently, Jakk no longer cared, but that was exactly what had destroyed them. Eric couldn't be anyone else's secret.

"Your silence isn't giving me hope."

Eric realized he had gotten lost in his thoughts. "I'm not sure what to do. A huge part of me wants to go with you, but I also don't want to go to Jakk's wedding. It doesn't feel right."

"Oh. Okay." Oakley sounded crestfallen. "I guess maybe I could call someone else."

Eric's throat swelled so fast and hard, he lost his breath. The idea of Oakley spending that weekend with someone else made him feel sick. He felt worse at the thought of Oakley on a date than he did knowing his ex was about to marry someone else. That was his big ex too. The one he was supposed to marry. It should have been his wedding.

"Exactly how much work would I have to miss?"

There was a pause—like he had shocked Oakley. "We could leave after you get off work that Friday. The wedding is on Saturday. Then we could head back home on Sunday. So, maybe two days."

"Hold on." Eric picked up his phone and found his employee app for work. He opened it and pulled up his schedule. "My days off are always different. It looks like I'm already off that Sunday and Monday. So, I'd only have to miss one day. I think Cheryl would probably let me off that day too."

"Are you being serious?" There was no missing the happiness in Oakley's voice. "Will you really go with me?"

Ugh. How was he supposed to say no? He covered his eyes and tried not to cringe. "Yeah. I'll go."

"Woot!"

A smile exploded across Eric's face at Oakley's shout. "Maybe don't get too excited. I'll likely get blackout drunk and cry, even though I'm over it. I'm just bitter about my current circumstances."

"I know." It sounded like Oakley was still smiling. "I swear I won't take it personally."

Eric didn't know why he would. They were just friends. Eric didn't mean anything to Oakley. He didn't mean anything to anyone. They had to talk about something else. "Tell me about your panels. I want to hear every detail." Eric enjoyed listening to Oakley talk about himself. The pride in his voice when he talked about his career and the game he loved made Eric forget about the ugliness of the world.

Eric closed his eyes and listened to the cadence of Oakley's voice. He blocked out everything else. In his head, he saw Oakley. His ridiculously light blue eyes always seemed to stare right into Eric's soul. They were at such odds with his dark hair. Eric intentionally kept his mind from thinking about the guy's amazing body. If Eric had been a different person, he would pursue Oakley like no one else ever had. But Eric was tired and used up. He had nothing to offer. There was a black hole where his heart used to be. It felt nice to have a friend, though. He had been alone for a long time, even when he had been with Jakk. For once, someone wanted his company. Eric would be there.

Chapter Two

To say Eric looked like he might be sick was a colossal understatement. Eric's dark hair was on point and his clothes were perfect for the event. But his dark blue eyes looked like a scared rabbit searching for an escape. It was painful to watch such a big, cuddly-looking guy look so unsure. Oakley didn't see any of the wedding from staring at Eric. He honestly didn't think Eric was upset about Jakk marrying someone else. It was like he expected to get attacked for simply being there. As far as Oakley could tell, no one had even looked their way. Unfortunately, that wasn't a trend that continued when they headed to the next banquet hall for the reception. Oakley immediately spotted two familiar faces headed their way.

Chipper was all smiles. The guy's light brown eyes always swam with good humor. He gave Oakley a one-arm hug. Luckily, he kept it light. Chipper was an MMA champion. His arms were deadly. His gaze moved over Oakley before jumping to Eric and back again, as if he fought to point out the obvious. Oakley had brought Jakk's ex to his wedding. "It's been forever, man. How have you been? Who is your friend?"

Oakley bit back a laugh. Chipper was a huge player. It hadn't occurred to him Chipper didn't know Eric. His quick inspection of Eric had nothing to do with him being Jakk's ex. The guy was always on the lookout for fresh meat. "This is Eric. Eric, Chipper."

Eric shook Chipper's hand. At least, he tried. Chipper brought Eric's hand to his mouth. "It's very nice to meet you."

Oakley exchanged a glance with Jayme. He assumed the two were there together, but Jayme was straight. Jayme was one of Jakk's teammates. A lot of athletes ran in the same circles. When Jayme's gaze met Oakley's, they rolled their eyes before going back to watching Chipper's sad attempt at seducing Eric.

Eric took his hand back and stepped closer to Oakley.

Oakley's chest swelled with pride. Maybe they weren't a couple, but it was nice to dream. He motioned toward Jayme. "This is Jayme. He—"

"Plays on Jakk's team," Eric finished for him. "We've met. Of course, you probably don't remember me, since I was *just a friend.*"

Eric didn't do a good job of hiding his bitterness with those air quotes.

Jayme didn't call him on it. "No. I remember. You were at one of our after parties. It's nice to see again."

"I'd very much appreciate if you would find your places at the dinner tables."

They all turned at the interruption. Oakley nearly snorted. He would recognize Baylor's snotty voice anywhere. The guy looked exactly like Oakley expected. He was ridiculously beautiful, as if polished by money. No doubt his services were astronomical.

Chipper was immediately distracted. "Well, hello. Who are you?" His gaze slid down Baylor's tiny body. He left no doubt he would do anything. Oakley might have found it hot had that look been directed at him, but he knew Chipper too well. He wasn't interested in that bullshit, and that was all a relationship with him would be.

Baylor looked every bit as uninterested. "Find. Your. Seat."

"Damn, sexy. I love a bossy man."

Green eyes narrowed on Chipper.

Chipper held up his hands in surrender. "We're going. Tell me your name, though."

Baylor walked away.

Chipper flashed Oakley an unrepentant smile. "I think he likes me. Do know who he is?"

Oakley shook his head at Chipper's ego. He couldn't even imagine what it must be like to be him. "Yeah. That's Baylor Keates. He's the wedding planner."

They headed for the tables. Chipper released a low whistle. "Damn. He put all this together? There must be five hundred people here."

Oakley nodded. It was impressive. They found their table and sat. Oakley was more than a little relieved when Chipper found his name card at a different table. Chipper was the type to monopolize the entire night. Oakley had asked Eric to join him for a reason. He wanted to spend time together.

Eric looked his way the instant they were seated. "Well, he's definitely something."

There was no denying that. "Yeah, but I imagine it takes a fuck-ton of confidence to become the MMA Light Heavyweight champion."

Eric's gaze slid toward the table where Chipper sat. Oakley followed his stare. As Oakley expected, he had everyone's attention. "There are a lot of athletes here."

Oakley took a drink of the tea in front of him. He winced. Oakley hated tea. "Yeah. Rocky has had a lot of clients over the years and met a lot of very talented athletes." He motioned for a nearby server. At least she had just dropped off plates at a different table, so he hoped she worked there.

She was all smiles as she rushed to his side. "How can I help?"

"How do we get a real drink around here?"

She motioned toward a line of bars set up around the room. "Visit any station and they'll help you out."

He nodded his thanks before focusing on Eric. "What would you like?"

Eric tried the tea. He immediately set it away from him. "Do you mind seeing if they have some sort of soda, or even just water? I'm not picky, but I can't drink that." He motioned toward his discarded glass.

"On it." He headed for the closest bar.

Jayme was already there, waiting for his drink. He flashed a smile at Oakley when he noticed him. "Hey. I take it you tried the tea?"

Oakley laughed. "Yeah. I'm more of a beer guy anyhow."

Jayme glanced toward the table where Oakley had left Eric. He looked as if he wanted to say something. Oakley wasn't surprised. He had been waiting for someone to be the first. "So, Jakk's ex, huh?"

"He's actually a really great guy." Oakley wanted to say more and defend Eric, but he didn't know how much Eric wanted people to know. He ordered a beer and a Coke.

"You know one reason he's no longer with Jakk is because he cheated, right?"

Oakley's gaze shot to Jayme. "Who? Jakk?" He wondered if Rocky knew that.

Jayme shook his head. "Eric. Rumor is he had someone else for more than a year before Jakk finally put him out."

"Oh." Oakley knew all about that, but he also knew something no one else did. It wasn't true. One night, when they had been deep in their cups, Eric had confessed he had done a lot of things, desperately trying to make Jakk get real about them. One thing had been pretending to see someone else, hoping the jealousy or even rage would shake up the situation Eric had found himself in. Being someone's dirty little secret was enough to break anyone. Oakley got it. It hadn't worked, though, and it was just one more thing Eric had to live with. It hurt Oakley's chest to see the way Eric punished himself even though he was the only one who got hurt. He wouldn't humiliate Eric by admitting the motives of a broken man.

"I'm not worried about that bullshit."

Jayme's gaze moved over Oakley's face, as if digging for the truth. "Okay. If you say so." Jayme took his drink and walked away.

Oakley rolled his eyes. He didn't need anyone to protect him. If anything, Eric was the one who needed to be warned. Oakley wasn't like Jakk. He had no shame when he wanted someone, and he wanted Eric. Eric's gorgeous face and sad soul had caught Oakley's attention. Anyone he had ever been with could attest. That wasn't a good thing. He didn't quit.

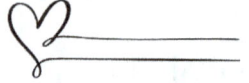

Eric had never wanted to go home so badly in his entire life. He felt like everyone watched him and judged him. Eric couldn't even find the will to get plastered. He worried a single drop of alcohol would make him puke... or cry. Either way, he would end up humiliated. Eric hated feeling judged. It upset him Oakley would ask him to do this. In fact, his paranoia had spread from everyone watching him to Oakley, setting him up for a huge bout of degradation. He was just so damn used to men fucking up his life. This entire situation was a nightmare.

"What happened to getting drunk and crying?"

Eric tried for a smile. He looked Oakley's way. Oakley had made the inquiry close to Eric's ear, where no one else could hear. When Eric turned his head, Oakley was still there. Eric had never been so close to him. His eyes were twice as beautiful inches away.

Eric forced himself to stay on topic. "I'm not in the mood to drink and I'm pretty sure I have no tears left to give."

Several people were dancing. A love song played, and Eric wanted to die.

"Would you like to head back to the room?"

Eric was on his feet and headed for the closest door before the question died on Oakley's lips. Oakley was hot on his heels. The walk to their hotel down the street was a silent one. Eric felt heavy. They had walked so they could get plastered. Now, Eric just felt empty and weak. He should have stayed, had a blast, and let the world see he hadn't been broken, but he had been. Eric didn't know how to put himself back together.

A loud, obnoxious-sounding wail escaped Oakley, making Eric jump in surprise. "You're not going to love me anymore after tonight. I made you come and now you hate me. Your silence says it all."

Oakley's act was so over the top that Eric could only stare and smile while Oakley pretended to melt down.

He grabbed Eric's arm and held on. "Please don't hate me. I have no other friends."

Eric laughed. "Bullshit."

Oakley turned sweetly serious. "But you're my best friend. No one matters the way you do."

Eric's eyes burned. He had to look away. It was true they spoke every single day for at least an hour at a time, but it hadn't really occurred to him that he might be the only person Oakley spoke to that often. But when he really thought about it, Oakley was his best friend too. He really didn't have anyone else.

Oakley linked fingers with him. "Seriously, I'm sorry I made you come. I never meant to cause you pain. There was just no way I could get out of this invitation and absolutely no one else I would come with."

He couldn't have Oakley thinking he caused Eric pain. "I'm not sorry. You're right. You're my best friend. If you suffer, I suffer. That's how it works."

A bark of laughter burst from Oakley. "Yeah. Weddings, in general, are pretty painful." He got serious. "It seems unmanly to admit it, but I thought I'd be married by now. I mean,

I'm thirty-six. Am I not supposed to be a settled adult by now? Fuck if I know."

Eric's chest hurt. "I understand. When I moved in with Jakk, I thought that's where my life was headed. Now, look at me. Further away than ever from having my picket fence."

"We should get married."

A nervous chuckle escaped Eric. "Cute."

"I'm being serious." He sounded like it. Eric couldn't deny that. "I like you way better than anyone else. You're always the first person I want to talk to in the morning and the last voice I want to hear every night. No one else matters like that to me. You could get out of your aunt's place, and quit, if you want. If you're not working, you can travel with me. We'd have a blast."

He was one hundred percent serious. Eric opened his mouth to say no. He didn't want to be trapped in a loveless marriage, but no words came out. Oakley's proposition was likely to be the only real chance he had of having a life.

Oakley bumped shoulders with him. "Come on. You want this. I can see it. You know we'd be happy."

Eric looked over.

Oakley looked strangely hopeful.

Eric didn't know what to say. "There's a lot we'd need to discuss. Like, I'm pretty sure you don't want to be celibate for the rest of your life, and I have no desire to be humiliated." Until he said the words, Eric didn't realize how badly he feared being the fool again. Maybe Jakk hadn't cheated, but he had betrayed Eric on every other level.

Oakley pulled him to a stop. He went toe to toe with Eric. They were the same height. Eric found that sexy. In fact, everything about Oakley appealed to him. Oakley shuffled closer, making Eric's heart beat a little faster. His expression screamed he would do bad things to Eric. Eric was ashamed to admit how badly he wanted that.

"I'm absolutely willing to share my bed with you and only you." Before Eric could process that new bit of information, Oakley kissed him. An inferno lit. They both moved closer, as if they couldn't stand an inch between them. Oakley held Eric's hips, staying respectful. Eric didn't want to be respected. He wanted to be touched. It had been so goddamn long since he felt anyone's hands on his body. He ached. Oakley's hard chest felt amazing beneath Eric's palms.

Oakley pulled away. His heated stare had Eric swallowing in nervousness. He would be intense and probably liked it rough. "We'll be fine in the bedroom department."

Eric forgot what they were talking about. "Yeah."

A triumphant-looking smile stretched Oakley's lips. "I'll make you proud to be my husband."

Goddamn. Had he just agreed to marry Oakley? He couldn't recall. His brain was too fuzzy. What the fuck? Oakley's gorgeous eyes never wavered from Eric. Eric realized he wanted this. There was absolutely nothing Oakley could take from him that Eric hadn't lost before. It didn't matter this wasn't love. This was better.

Chapter Three

THE SILENT INNER PANIC was thick. Oakley could see it in Eric's eyes and feel it in the air. He had no intention of giving Eric time and space. Oakley had him on the ropes. Eric had agreed to marry him, which was completely insane. He wasn't oblivious to that. That didn't mean Oakley planned to stop. Everything amazing that had ever happened in his life was due to Oakley jumping in with both feet and no fear. That was why he knew this marriage would be no different from every other success he had achieved.

He watched Eric peel off his dress jacket and take off his tie. Next went the dress shirt, leaving behind nothing but the white T-shirt beneath. Fuck. Eric was sexy. Eric had thick, toned arms that showed he lifted weights, but he had a stomach that proved he liked to eat. Goddamn. That was exactly Oakley's type. He would fuck Oakley hard and then cuddle afterward. Oakley practically whimpered with unquenched need. He hadn't touched anyone else since Eric caught his eye. Now he was dying.

Eric looked his way and caught him staring. A shy smile appeared. "What?"

Oakley shook his head. "You're incredibly gorgeous."

A blush tinted Eric's cheeks. He looked away. "Uh. Thanks. You too."

Oakley shook his head. He fought a laugh. "I'm going to grab a quick shower. Do you need in there first?"

Eric shook his head while keeping his gaze locked on his bag.

Oakley didn't know if he actually hunted for something or if he just avoided Oakley's stare. Either way, Oakley decided to give him a little space. As he walked toward the bathroom, Eric suddenly stepped into his path. Oakley didn't get a chance to guess at his intentions. The air was knocked from his lungs as his back hit the bed. Eric's huge body covered his. His tongue filled Oakley's mouth. Oakley moaned. It was out of his control. He had known this person was inside Eric. Jakk had mentally beaten him down, but the real Eric was still in there. Oakley saw him now.

Eric shoved his hand beneath Oakley and squeezed his ass as he ground down on him. Oakley nearly came in his pants. Eric kneaded as he rocked against Oakley, stealing his every thought. Their tongues fought as Oakley tore at Eric's skin. Eric made no move to get Oakley out of his clothes. Oakley was ready to beg.

Eric's mouth moved to Oakley's ear. "Tell me how to please you. I'm not a bottom."

Thank fucking god. "Good. I am."

Eric froze. He pulled away just enough to stare down at Oakley. "I never would've guessed that."

Oakley got it. He knew he didn't give off that vibe, but he loved to get fucked. He wanted it now. Oakley held Eric's stare. "Now you know. Get inside me."

Eric sat back on his heels and peeled off his t-shirt. He had a hairy chest. Oakley's stomach muscles clenched. He couldn't remember wanting anyone as badly. Everything he had said earlier was the truth. Oakley felt closer to Eric than anyone else in the world. There was no one else he wanted to be with. He didn't think Eric realized how hard it was to be Oakley's friend. Oakley was never around. He was always traveling. Being his friend meant always bending to his schedule. Eric never even seemed to notice how much he met Oakley more than halfway all the time. Honestly, that made him kind of sad. That meant Eric was so used to being unimportant to people he didn't even think about it anymore. Oakley had to take care of him. He wanted Eric to travel with him and be first in his life, but he knew—after the way Jakk had strung him along for years—Eric would never agree to be that guy without marriage. If Oakley was to ever marry anyone, it would be Eric, so he had thrown it out there. Now he couldn't stop thinking about how badly he wanted Eric tied to him. Oakley couldn't be on Eric's dick fast enough. He had never felt so needy in his life.

Oakley worked on tearing his way out of his shirt. His eyes stayed locked on Eric unbuttoning and unzipping his pants. Oakley tried twisting from side to side to take off his dress shirt, but aggravation built with each passing second. He growled in frustration. His gaze met Eric's. They held each other's stare for a moment. Smiles exploded across their faces as if they realized at the same time exactly how much the other wanted this and how crazy the entire situation was. Eric rolled to his back and scrambled from his pants and underwear while Oakley stripped as quickly as possible. Eric's bag was still on the end of the bed. He snagged it, found the toiletries bag inside, and fished around until he came out with a condom and a small thing of lube.

He met Oakley's stare again. "Don't worry. This was already in there. I didn't plan this."

Oakley snorted without thinking. He immediately explained. "You're not that guy, and I'm pretty sure I started us down this road." He raked a heated gaze down Eric's body, catching sight of his huge erection before meeting Eric's stare again. Oakley let Eric see his lust. "You should hurry."

While still holding his gaze, Eric brought the condom to his lips and ripped into the package with his teeth. Oakley was pretty sure he panted. His mind wasn't working clearly any longer. Eric rolled the condom down his length. Oakley snatched up the lube and went to work, readying himself. Things weren't moving fast enough for him. The instant he thought he was wet enough, he attacked. Oakley shoved Eric onto his back and straddled him. He impaled himself on Eric's cock. His gaze collided with

Eric's. Time froze. It hit Oakley exactly how desperate he was for them to be more. He would do anything. Somewhere in the past year, Eric had become everything to him. He couldn't fuck this up.

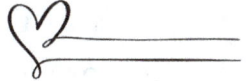

Somewhere along the line, Eric had lost his confidence. The way Oakley looked at him gave that self-assurance back to him. Oakley wanted him. Not just a little. Oakley acted desperate to have him. That was a mind fuck and an ego stroke. For a moment, it was like the universe held its breath. Oakley was on his dick, and they stared into each other's eyes. Eric made a monumental discovery. He felt a hell of a lot more than he had wanted to admit to himself. Eric had been holding back, pretending all he wanted was friendship. Fuck that. He wanted everything.

Eric rolled, pinning Oakley beneath him, and took what he craved. The more he thrust, the harder he went. Oakley moaned like he loved it, and Eric's brain was in a fog. The problem was, he wasn't going to last. It had truly been forever since he had sex. Oakley had his head a mess and his body on fire. He was about to disappoint the fuck out of Oakley.

Calling on every ounce of strength he possessed, Eric pulled out and slithered down Oakley's body. He swallowed Oakley's erection. A shout burst from Oakley as Eric took him all the way down his throat. It was no small feat and his throat burned, but he meant business. Eric was horny as hell and on the edge. He didn't want to play. Eric needed Oakley to blow so he could without humiliating himself.

Oakley grabbed his hair and held on. "Fuck, Eric. You're killing me. Goddamn. That feels good."

He was still talking too much. Eric needed him incoherent. He fingered Oakley's asshole, finding that hot button inside. He massaged as he bobbed on Oakley's cock. Oakley squirmed and whined while trying to fuck Eric's fingers. He felt Oakley tense. Eric shot forward and impaled him once again. Oakley blew. His back arched, and he scratched Eric's skin. Oakley's orgasm took Eric out. He gasped and cried out against Oakley's chest, riding the pulses of Oakley's orgasm. His mind was completely blank. Ecstasy ruled the moment. He saw heaven and hell. Eric felt all the emotions from the high of Oakley to realization of how much this would hurt someday. He had shut himself off from his emotions, and now they were wide open again. Oakley was already under his skin. He was fucking terrified.

Oakley ran his fingers through Eric's hair.

Eric kept his face pressed to Oakley's chest. To his horror, there were tears in his eyes. Eric hadn't expected this. Oakley had shown up out of the blue and taken over his life. He hadn't meant to feel anything for him beyond friendship.

"I know." Oakley lifted Eric's chin and lured him into a kiss. His lips skimmed Eric's. "Me too." He brushed another light kiss across Eric's mouth. "I didn't see you coming, but I'm so goddamn thankful."

Eric took the kiss he wanted. He needed to taste whatever budded between them. Happiness felt odd, but that was what grew in his heart. He found himself chuckling against Oakley's lips. There was no place for all his hope and joy to go. "You probably want that shower."

Oakley pressed his forehead against Eric's shoulder and shook with laughter. If Oakley was serious about marrying him, then Eric was in. Their marriage would be built on friendship. That sounded like stability to him.

Chapter Four

LIFE WAS STRANGE AS fuck. When Eric had abandoned his college career to join Jakk on his professional football journey, he had enjoyed decorating their new home. For years, he had been surrounded by the lap of luxury. He had free access to Jakk's millions and could do anything he wanted, except the only thing he wanted: love Jakk openly.

Now Eric couldn't make himself look too closely at the ridiculously expensive high-rise apartment in the middle of New York where Oakley lived. Where Eric lived now too. Fuck. How exactly had that happened? Rather than eyeing the amazing view or sleek modern... everything, Eric chose to inspect Oakley's shrine to himself. Eric knew that wasn't what it was. Honestly, it was just a room housing awards and souvenirs of his long, successful career. It was just fucking strange. The past couple of years had been a complete rollercoaster for him. His highs and lows had been as extreme as they got. He felt like he walked through a dream.

Oakley plopped down on the chaise end of the couch in his shrine room. He supposed it was more of a man cave. Oakley tossed a baseball into the air, catching it over and over while he watched Eric.

"Do you like baseball? It just occurred to me I've never really asked that."

Eric flashed him a smile. "I don't dislike it. It's just not a sport I ever paid much attention to before meeting you. I don't completely understand all the rules yet."

Oakley set his ball aside and patted the spot between his legs.

It was a summons Eric had no trouble obeying. He sat between Oakley's thighs and leaned back against his chest.

Oakley kissed the shell of his ear. "I thought it would take longer to move in all your stuff. I thought you'd have... stuff."

Eric laughed. It was true. All Eric owned were a few bags of clothes and a couple of odds and ends. Nothing, really. Everything he once owned actually belonged to Jakk. He didn't know how to stop being bitter over that. "Yeah, well. When I told you I lost everything, I meant it." His confession was met with silence. He wished he hadn't said anything. If Oakley had any big exes, he never talked about them. Eric needed to learn to extend him the same respect. He just wasn't used to them being more than friends yet.

"Damn. For Rocky's sake, I really wanted to like Jakk. The more I hear, the harder that is."

Eric shrugged. "He is a good person. Everyone is the villain in someone's story. I imagine I'm his too. Not that any of that matters anymore."

Oakley's lips moved to Eric's neck. "It's okay for it to matter. Your past made you who you are, and I'm pretty fucking fond of who you are. In fact." Oakley squirmed behind him as if trying to find something. His arms encircled Eric again. He popped open a velvet box.

Eric's chin dropped. His eyes burned at the sight of the black band with gold etchings. He couldn't tear his eyes away from it.

"Obviously, when I asked you to marry me, it was kind of spontaneous. I didn't even think about a ring until we got back home. But you deserve to have all the traditional hoopla, including an engagement ring. I have no idea if it'll fit." With his chin resting on Eric's shoulder, he pulled the ring from the box and put it on Eric's finger. It fit. It was a little loose, but that made it perfect. Eric couldn't stand tight jewelry.

He swallowed past the lump in his throat. "Thank you. It's gorgeous."

He felt Oakley shrug. "It's supposed to resemble some kind of king's crown. I don't know. They tried to explain it to me. All I knew was it looked perfect for you. Well, us. There's a matching one for me for the ceremony."

He was so fucking serious about this marriage, and goddamn if that wasn't exactly what Eric needed. Oakley was a healing balm on years of resentment. Each day, things felt realer, and Eric got a little more excited.

"I wish I had thought to buy yours. That seems like the thing to do."

Oakley blew out a raspberry, making Eric laugh. "To me, the ring isn't as important as the actual marriage. A ring is just spending money. Money doesn't buy happiness."

That was something Eric fully knew. Still. "It's easy to say that when you have money."

Oakley didn't laugh like he hoped. Instead, he sounded serious when he responded. "You have money now too." Before Eric could respond or argue, Oakley moved on. "Now, how big do you want this wedding to be? I want to hire that Baylor guy. I've already left a message for him to call me to discuss it. He had that shit down to a science at Rocky's wedding. Not that I imagine our ceremony being as insane as theirs."

Eric was dumbfounded. He had honestly assumed Oakley would want to get married quietly with just the two of them. Planning a full-on wedding hadn't been on his bingo card for the year. He cleared his throat. "Um, I guess it depends on when you want to get married and who you want to invite. I don't really have anyone. My mom is in memory care back in California. She doesn't even know who I am any longer. Otherwise, there's just my aunt. My side will look pretty depressing." He didn't want to add he didn't have friends. After Jakk, Eric literally had nothing and no one.

"Hmm." Oakley sounded thoughtful. "I went to this wedding when I was a kid. We waited at our tables in the reception hall, with the adults getting the jump on the open bar, while the couple were married in private in the next room. Apparently, it was some old tradition on one of their families' sides. Something about couples who didn't show off their love had the longest and strongest marriages. Anyhow, for a kid, it was great. I didn't have to sit through the wedding part. We went straight to the eating and dancing when the couple walked through the door. I remember everyone cheering, and then they started serving food."

Eric mulled it over. On one hand, he loved the idea of not having his side of the venue empty and feeling subconscious while walking down the aisle in front of strangers. On the other hand, he kind of wanted the world to see him marry such a great guy. An idea struck. "What if we live-streamed the wedding in the reception hall? That way, people can get a jumpstart on drinking and watch, if they want."

"Love it." Oakley's mouth opened on the side of his neck. He sucked.

Eric's eyes fell closed as he savored the way chill bumps formed on his skin. He had been hyper aware of his loneliness every second for years now. A shaky-sounding breath escaped him. Oakley's palm flattened against Eric's chest over his heart. He pulled Eric even closer as he nibbled on his skin. His hand headed south. Eric held his breath. Oakley found the hem of his shirt and dipped underneath. He stroked Eric's stomach and chest.

"Everything about you is sexy as hell."

Eric's eyes burned. There was no way Oakley understood how much he needed everything he did and said. "I've never been so thankful for anyone in my life." That was as close as Eric could come to explaining the emotions roiling inside him.

Oakley's phone rang. He growled against Eric's skin before snagging the nearby device and checking the face. "Oh, hey. It's Baylor." He pressed the phone to his ear. "Hello?" Oakley paused. "Yeah. Eric and I would love to discuss hiring you to plan our wedding. What's the fastest you've ever set up a medium-sized gathering?"

Something evil rose in Eric. He turned and moved to his knees before tugging Oakley down on the couch. Eric wasted no time tearing open the front of Oakley's pants.

Oakley's eyes burned with lust and the threat of retribution. Eric looked forward to his revenge. For now, he wanted to suck dick.

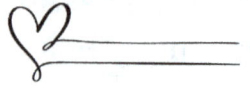

Sinister. Oakley tried to breathe quietly as Eric took him to the back of his throat. It was damn hard to answer Baylor's questions with Eric's hot mouth tugging at his cock.

"How medium-sized are we talking?"

Oakley drew a slow breath through his nose. "Um. Maybe a third of Rocky's ceremony. Would it speed things up if I said the vow exchange will be private and live streamed so your focus will mostly be on the reception?"

Eric pulled some move with his tongue that had Oakley violently swallowing a moan.

"If you're fine with a very basic decorative style—like plain white plates and tablecloths, and simple flower arrangements—I could pull something together in a matter of days. Of course, that depends heavily on the location. If you want a popular venue, those can book out years in advance."

Oakley moved the phone away for a second so he could breathe through a pant. He desperately fought to keep talking. Oakley went back to his call. "We're not picky about any of that. If you have some ideas and would like to set up something to go over all the options, that would be amazing."

"Sure. I have an appointment open tomorrow around two. Will that work?"

"That's perfect." He ran his fingers through Eric's hair. He was so close to being free to punish him.

"Would you like me to list my fees before you feel like I wasted your time?"

"Nope." Oakley struggled hard. "Money doesn't matter when it comes to Eric."

Eric's head shot up.

Their gazes met.

Baylor said something about true love being adorable.

Oakley somehow managed a goodbye. Then his tongue battled with Eric's. He had Eric's pants down just enough to get what he wanted. Eric's huge body covered his and Eric held their dicks together as he stroked. There was a massive amount of need driving him insane. He knew he was moving with Eric at lightning speed. Oakley needed Eric tied to him before Eric came to his senses. He had always been the type to know what he wanted and go after it with everything he had. It was more than that, though. There was a lot Eric didn't know about him.

He knew—if and when Eric realized those things—he would leave Oakley in the dust.

Pressure climbed Oakley's shaft. He dug his fingertips into Eric's skin as he fought to fly. Oakley bit Eric's lip, turning frantic beneath him. He was so close to what Eric's touch offered. When the first burst of ecstasy stole the air from his lungs, the biggest reason for his rush looked clearer than ever. Baylor wasn't wrong. Somewhere along the line in the past year, Oakley had fallen in love with Eric, and it was adorable. He couldn't lose him. Oakley couldn't go back to being alone. He needed this too much.

Chapter Five

WEDDING PLANNING MOVED BLESSEDLY quick. The options Baylor had for fast and simple weddings were still gorgeous. Plus, there was a huge wedding chapel one town over that stayed put together and had an open day just two weeks out. The place was a combination wedding venue and reception hall. Since they recorded every wedding as part of their package, live streaming was a breeze. Baylor impressed the hell out of Oakley with how fast he threw everything together without stressing them at all. Everything went on behind the scenes with very little input needed from them. Of course, his fee matched his worth. Oakley never stressed about that. However, he had fully expected a hate-filled call from Rocky when he received the wedding invitation. To his surprise, all he got was radio silence. If he RSVP'd, Oakley wouldn't know. Baylor kept watch over the numbers.

Then he stood facing Eric, with a camera recording every moment, and everything suddenly felt very, very real. He was hyper aware of everyone watching one room over until Eric smiled. Oakley forgot everything except the man who had agreed to do this absolutely insane thing with him.

"You're completely crazy. You know that, right?"

Eric laughed. "So are you."

Oakley shook his head. "Nah. I know exactly what I'm doing and I've never been happier."

The way Eric turned dewy-eyed at the confession made it worthwhile.

"Let's begin."

Oakley focused on the officiator. The bald man was elaborately dressed in silky robes. Oakley had never subscribed to religion. Honestly, he never even thought much about it. People were born and then they died. It all seemed cut and dry to him. He supposed people were scared of dying and needed a storybook afterlife. Oakley didn't understand that. He imagined death was like falling asleep. It seemed crazy to fear sleeping. Truthfully, they wouldn't be scared if someone hadn't taught them they would burn for eternity if they weren't perfect in everyone else's eyes. It felt a little like they caused their own anxiety. He knew he focused on random thoughts to avoid being scared shitless. Eric could still say no. Then what? He would be humiliated, but worse than that, he would be completely heartbroken.

Oakley blinked, and he was repeating his vows. Eric looked every bit as scared as Oakley until they both said "I do." Then he looked at Oakley in a way Oakley had been begging the universe for—like he loved him.

"I now pronounce you bound for life. You may kiss to seal your love for eternity."

Now they were at the good part. Oakley overcame Eric and kissed him like he couldn't wait to find the nearest flat surface. He heard the cheer ring out from the reception hall. Eric smiled against his lips. They burst out laughing. Oakley had never been so happy. Hand in hand, they headed to join the party. As they cleared the door, everyone came to their feet and clapped. Whistles filled the air. They had chosen not to do assigned seating. The only reserved table was theirs. Oakley spotted Rocky and Jakk as they passed. They were deep in conversation with Chipper, so Oakley couldn't get a read on their thoughts. But they had shown, and that was something.

Eric followed his line of sight and squeezed his hand. "Are you worried he won't want to stay friends?"

Oakley focused on his new husband. "No. You're worth more to me than that." He truly was, but Oakley was still slightly worried. Rocky was more than his friend. He was his agent. Rocky should have dropped him after Oakley retired. There was no reason for Rocky to keep finding ways to keep Oakley relevant, especially now. The guy wasn't making any money off Oakley's little conventions. Oakley worried over it while trying to focus on their night. When they stood to mingle after dinner, he was more than a little relieved when Rocky and Jakk immediately headed their way. Jakk had a middle-aged woman on his arm. She was all smiles, walking between Jakk and Eric's aunt.

Eric froze.

Oakley glanced over. There were tears in his eyes.

"Mom."

Her smile grew.

Eric covered his mouth.

It hit Oakley. Jakk had set it up for Eric's mom to be there, and the miracle of miracles, she actually remembered him tonight.

Eric sniffed and closed the distance between them. He hugged his mom, squeezing her until Oakley was certain she couldn't breathe.

Rocky pulled Oakley's attention his way. "His aunt says she's been having some good days lately. So Jakk talked to his mom, who lives nearby, and set it up for her to make the trip with her. We colluded with Baylor, so it would be a surprise."

Oakley shook his head. He couldn't stop watching Eric cry and hug his mom. "I should've thought to do this, but all Eric ever says is she doesn't remember him anymore."

Rocky squeezed his shoulder. "Just see it as the gift it is. You look really happy. I was honestly beyond confused when I got your invitation, but then I watched your vow exchange. That was love I saw. I guess I've been a little too wrapped up in my own life to notice some things. This is definitely a story I'd like to hear, though."

Oakley chuckled. "Yeah. It's not really that in-depth. I confronted him about stalking you and learned he wasn't. He actually lived in New York and had a reason to be there. It truly was just an odd coincidence for you two to be in the same place at the same time. So I sat and talked with him for a while. It turns out he's incredible."

Rocky nodded. "Yeah. It didn't take me long to figure out it wasn't him trying to get between Jakk and me. Unfortunately, it's someone who's still very much around. I can only hope he's done with his bullshit."

Oakley lifted his eyebrows in question.

Rocky shook his head. "It's a long story, and this is your wedding. You should meet your mother-in-law before she relapses."

With a nod, Oakley happily joined his husband. He met Jakk's gaze as he passed. "Thank you." He mouthed the words so he wouldn't disturb Eric's conversation with his mom.

Jakk dipped his chin. "Congratulations," he mouthed back, easing something in Oakley's chest. He didn't care how Jakk felt about him or his marriage, but again, Rocky mattered to him. That meant Jakk was relevant by association. Plus, it was just better for everyone for Jakk and Eric to bury the hatchet and let the past be the past. Oakley was Eric's future. He planned to make it like a dream come true. Jakk no longer mattered.

Eric's emotions were all over the place. His mom hadn't gotten to stay long before Jakk's mom took her back to their hotel for the night. Eric knew it was for the best. She was having a good moment, but when that ended, she would likely melt down. That was a heartache Eric didn't want at his wedding. He had suffered it too many times over the years.

Oakley held him while they enjoyed their first dance as a married couple. Reality didn't feel very real, and Eric walked on clouds. When they had exchanged vows, Oakley had stared at Eric like he loved him. Eric was scared as hell to dream. He knew they were married, and this should be forever, but that didn't mean Oakley had to love him. Eric wanted him to, though.

"Thank you."

Oakley's words caught Eric off guard. "For what?"

"Marrying me, obviously," Eric said with a laugh. "You could've had anyone."

Oakley was always saying things like that, and Eric didn't understand. Between the two of them, Oakley was definitely the prize. "I should be thanking you. Before you stormed my table at that sports bar, I didn't think I would ever be happy." Eric leaned back enough to hold Oakley's stare. "I didn't think I'd ever feel like this again." He prayed Oakley understood and didn't make him say the words. Eric couldn't be the first. He had been crushed too hard by life. Oakley was all he had. If Oakley didn't feel the same, Eric couldn't hear him say it. He would still do his damnedest to make this the happiest of all marriages, but it would hurt. Eric didn't know how much more pain he could take.

Oakley didn't shy away. His gaze never wavered. "Rocky says he saw the love between us when we said our vows."

Damn. They were really trying to wait each other out, inching toward the same goal.

Eric just didn't know if he could stand to be wrong.

Thankfully, Oakley didn't leave things at that. "He's always been the smartest person in the room."

Eric's heart soared. A smile exploded across his face. "Sounds like it."

Oakley never lost his intensity. He touched his lips to Eric's. Eric's breath caught at the sweetness of his kiss. "So, thank you," Oakley repeated. "You're everything I dreamed I would have someday. I just never realized how much I would love you."

Eric's eyes burned. His throat swelled. "It'll kill me if you stop." He couldn't stop the confession. Oakley was uniquely positioned to wreck him in a way he couldn't survive. Eric's heart and sanity were held together by cardboard and cheap masking tape that already curled at the edges. One blow and he was done. Oakley had no clue how much trust Eric showed in him. He had nothing left to take.

"Same." Oakley sounded so genuine—like he truly counted on Eric's love to get out of bed each day. It was odd. As far as he knew or had seen, Oakley had no reason to easily break. But sometimes Oakley showed Eric glimpses of something dark. Eric wanted all of him, even the secretly broken pieces. He had to start somewhere. Eric had to be vulnerable too.

"I love you."

Oakley looked away for a second. Eric thought he saw tears well in Oakley's eyes, but he was too quick. When he looked back, Eric's breath caught in his throat. Oakley honestly looked like he might cry. "I love you too."

It hit Eric. For some unknown reason, all his own, Oakley didn't think he was worthy of love. Oakley missed a step, and a tremor ran through him. Eric immediately pulled him in closer and kept him steady.

"I've got you." The last few whirlwind weeks had been exhausting. Amazing but draining. Eric had size, if nothing else. He could be the strength for once. That's what marriage was, shoring up each other through every aspect of existence. They would have a gorgeous life. Eric knew it in his heart.

Chapter Six

IT WAS SEXY WATCHING Oakley on the field. Eric would take it to the grave, but he maybe had a thing for athletes. Their competitive nature and do anything to win attitude. The sexy way their bodies moved while flexing a perfectly honed talent. A shiver ran through Eric. Goddamn. He couldn't wait to get Oakley home. First, Oakley had to win this game. The game was just some charity softball thing with a bunch of celebrity players. It wasn't only baseball players involved, but soccer, football, and hockey too. There was an interesting mixture of people, and it was for a good cause, so how could Oakley say no? Eric tried to ignore the fact that Jakk was also on the field. They were mostly okay, especially after Jakk bringing his mom to the wedding, but it was still strange to be in his sphere. He hated to admit how kind Jakk's gesture had been. That move truly proved how long and well they knew each other. It was something a real friend would do. It was the exact move Eric needed to completely leave the hard feelings in the past. They were better off without each other. Sometimes, life just took some turns to get to fate.

With the game being played in Southern California, Oakley had insisted they come early so they could visit Eric's mom. Every day, Eric fell a little more in love with him. They had only been married a month, but every second had been perfect. He hadn't known life could feel this way.

Rocky leaned his way. "You look happy."

Eric had forgotten he was there. He had been so focused on Oakley, everything else had disappeared. Eric flashed him a smile. "I am." He had a thought he hadn't considered until he had seen the way Oakley worried over Rocky's reaction to their marriage. Still, he hesitated before deciding just to talk about it. "I hope you don't feel like Oakley was hiding anything from you."

A sweet smile touched Rocky's lips. He truly was a handsome guy. Eric saw what Jakk saw in him, as strange as that was to admit. "Nah. Oakley has always been someone who plays things close to the chest. As much as I consider him a good friend, I'm still not sure I even know him."

That was a very fitting description. Eric had silently fallen in love with Oakley. It had happened so quietly, mostly because Oakley could be so closed to the world around him.

Eric had never seen his love coming. "Yeah. I'm not sure why he's like that. He loves hard. He just doesn't let people in."

With his gaze locked on the game, Rocky nodded. "I imagine it's because of his dad. You know he had all that tough guy, men don't have feelings attitude, and raised his son to be a real man. The guy's a dick, which I'm sure you know."

Eric hadn't known. Oakley never talked about his parents. Eric had asked, but Oakley had only said they didn't talk. When he had tried to dig, Oakley had just smiled and nicely asked him to stop. He never brought up the topic again. It hurt his feelings a little that Rocky knew something he didn't about Oakley's past, but they had known each of for several years. Eric couldn't compete with that. Rocky likely knew a mountain of things Eric didn't.

"I think I owe you an apology," Rocky said suddenly, surprising Eric.

"Why?" Seriously. He had no clue why Rocky thought he owed Eric anything.

An uncomfortable-sounding chuckle fell from Rocky's lips. "When Jakk and I first got together, I thought you were trying to split us up. I'm the reason Oakley spilled that beer on you."

Eric laughed. "He told me. Don't be sorry. If that hadn't happened, I wouldn't be happily married now. Sometimes life is funny, but fate is rarely wrong."

Rocky turned his head and held his stare. "Still, I feel bad for thinking badly of you. Not just anyone could handle what you do. Jakk says, after taking care of your mom until the second you literally couldn't anymore, he never dreamed you'd marry someone else with a chronic illness."

Eric's blood ran cold.

Rocky kept talking like he hadn't dropped an atomic bomb on Eric's life. "I realize Oakley's MS is still in the beginning stages now, but he could very well end up in a wheelchair. You saw all that and still chose him. Despite everything with Jakk, I think you must be an amazing person and you deserved better from me."

First off, considering Rocky had married his ex, that was the nicest fucking thing in the world. Now Eric felt bad for ever hating him. Secondly, what the fuck? He scrambled to say something, anything, while his brain tried catching up. For pride's sake, he couldn't let Rocky know he hadn't known. Eric cleared his throat. Thankfully, he just sounded uncomfortable with the topic and not ignorant as hell. "I love him. That's all that matters." There. Fuck. Eric's gaze moved back to the field and latched on to Oakley. His mind raced as he went over every second together. There were signs. He should have noticed and questioned some things. But Oakley was damn good at making excuses and laughing about being a klutz. Plus, Eric had no reason to doubt him. Unfortunately, he saw it now. The rigid moments when Oakley had trouble moving. He blamed it on too many years of professional sports. Any time Eric saw him tremble, his brain automatically blamed anything and everything else.

Oakley's head turned. Their gazes met. A sexy smile stretched Oakley's lips. He winked. Goddamn it. Jakk was right. Eric probably wouldn't have chosen to take care of anyone ever again. The mental drain of his mother's care had nearly killed him. But Eric hadn't lied. He loved Oakley. They were through sickness and health until death parted them. Eric blew out a slow breath. He would take care of Oakley. He felt too much to ever walk away.

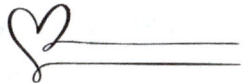

Everything hurt. One of these days, Oakley would have to give up doing these charity games. For now, the exercise was good for him, and he wasn't ready to surrender. He also kind of adored seeing Eric watching him. Oakley had never had anyone he loved cheer for him. Before Oakley publicly came out, his dad had come to games, proud to have raised a man's man. That stopped the moment Oakley became an embarrassment. Maybe this was just a softball game. Nothing like his pro baseball. Still, he knew someone was there for him who loved him for him. He was scared shitless it was only temporary.

A thousand times, Oakley had almost told Eric the truth. Then he would think about how bad things would likely get and his tongue would freeze. He wasn't ready to watch Eric walk away—the way people always did when he stopped being perfect in their eyes. Oakley wanted more memories with Eric. One of these days, he would have to let him go. For now, though, Oakley wanted as much time as he could get with his husband. Having a spouse mattered to him. He hated the idea of not waking up in Eric's arms. Oakley didn't know how to lose that, but he also couldn't expect Eric to give up his adult years to take care of him the way he had given up his youth for his mom. That wasn't fair. Oakley loved him too much to burden him.

"You're being awful quiet."

Oakley looked up from packing his suitcase. They would head home in the morning. He liked being prepared, so he didn't leave anything behind. "Sorry. I guess I'm just tired. It's been a while since I played. I'm out of shape," he added, forcing a chuckle.

Eric closed the distance between them. He wrapped his arms around Oakley and made a show of stroking his body. "You don't feel out of shape to me."

Oakley's smile turned real. Eric made it impossible for him to mope. "You're biased."

"No... maybe, but I'm also not blind. I assure you, you're sexy as hell."

In spite of himself, Oakley's smile slipped. "That's probably all I have going for me." And it wouldn't last forever. His body probably wouldn't last five more years before he started to really deteriorate.

Eric scowled. "Don't say shit like that. I didn't fall in love with your looks. I fell in love with your heart. This marriage is forever. Do you plan to leave me when I start looking old? Or what if I'm in a horrific car crash and end up deformed and paralyzed? Will that change how you feel about me?"

Even though Eric sounded truly enraged, Oakley snorted at the stupidity of the question. "You're the most incredible person I've ever met. Why would I care how you look?"

Eric gave him a sharp nod. "Exactly. Stop being dumb."

For a second, Oakley swore Eric knew everything. His outrage was too genuine to be hypothetical, but there was no way. Unfortunately, this discussion was completely theoretical. Eric would feel differently when he learned the truth. Still, for now, he was at Oakley's side. He appreciated it more than words could say.

"You're perfect."

"No." Eric shook his head. He looked serious. "Not even in the slightest, but I love being your husband. I'd rather be with you than be anywhere at all. You're not getting rid of me."

Oakley's throat swelled. He couldn't respond, even if he had any words. All Oakley had was actions. He pulled Eric closer and skimmed his lips across Eric's mouth. Oakley did it again until Eric took charge and claimed his mouth. Oakley shoved, taking Eric down on the bed. Eric laughed as Oakley tore at the front of his jeans. Oakley had to taste him. He loved his husband's flavor. In no time, he had Eric's cock in his mouth.

"Shit."

Oakley wanted to pat himself on the back for the surprised wonder in Eric's voice. He put his heart and soul into sucking Eric's dick.

Eric tugged at his shirt. "Let me have them clothes. Flip around here. I want to get you off."

Oakley ignored him and doubled his efforts. This was about Eric. Oakley wasn't useless yet. He could still make Eric fly. The desperate sounds Eric made, and the way he fought to fuck Oakley's mouth, were like crack. Oakley never wanted to stop. He was fully addicted. When a shout rent the air and cum filled his mouth, tears welled in Oakley's eyes. He swallowed before burying his face against Eric's stomach. Oakley wanted to rage against life, screaming how unfair everything was. But Oakley saw Eric for the blessing he was, and this bullshit was no one's fault. He just wished—for once—he would get to keep someone who loved him. Oakley was tired as hell of being alone in the world. Just the one time, he needed more.

Chapter Seven

KICKED BACK ON THE couch with Eric's head in his lap while watching a movie was Oakley's happy place. He was completely at peace. His hands trembled a bit tonight, but he kept them busy, running his fingers through Eric's hair.

"You're putting me to sleep."

Eric's groggy voice made him smile. "That's okay."

Eric rolled and stared up at Oakley. "Do you want to move to the bedroom and finish the movie in there? That way, we can cuddle, and if I fall asleep, then I'm already in bed."

"Sure." Oakley loved the cuddling suggestion. "I just need a quick shower."

With a nod, Eric rolled from the couch. Oakley pushed the button to lower the footrest. His leg felt stiff, but the slow movement gave him time to adjust. It hurt like hell when he pushed to his feet. He didn't do a good job of hiding his wince or the stumble that followed.

Eric's arm shot out, steadying him. The concern etched on his face made Oakley feel sick. "Are you okay?"

Oakley worked up a fake smile. "Yeah. I guess I didn't realize how hard I went during this morning's workout." He tried to laugh it off. If Eric believed, Oakley would never know. Eric had looked away before Oakley got a read on him.

"Okay." Eric headed for the bedroom like nothing happened.

Oakley bit back a sigh of relief and followed. He fought not to limp. Tonight was bad. It was a good thing he had a doctor's appointment tomorrow.

While Eric turned back the covers and turned on the TV, Oakley headed for the safety of the bathroom. He needed to get out of sight. Hopefully, the hot water would loosen up his body. Oakley stood under the scalding water for much longer than usual. He even turned on the steam feature he never used. It was hard as hell, keeping Eric in the dark. He didn't know how long he could. Eric wasn't dumb. Eventually, he would have questions.

Oakley reluctantly turned off the water. He had already spent a suspiciously long time in the bathroom. He didn't want Eric to worry. Of course, it was equally possible Eric had already gone to sleep. Cold air washed over Oakley's overheated skin when he stepped from the shower. His leg immediately locked, knocking him off balance. He was too wet to catch himself on anything and smacked face down on the bathroom floor. It hurt. Every inch of the front side of his body had taken the full impact.

To his horror, the bathroom door flew open. "Holy shit, Oakley."

"I'm okay."

Eric looked ready to call an ambulance as he pulled Oakley to his feet. He shuffled him back into the shower to the bench inside. "Sit. Fuck. Are you hurt?"

A nervous chuckle escaped Oakley. "Just my pride." Truthfully, everything hurt. Bruises were already forming.

Eric turned on the water again, obviously uncaring of the shorts he still wore. He grabbed the body wash. "Come on. I know if I found myself on the bathroom floor, I'd definitely want a shower repeat. No matter how clean the floor is."

Oakley sat there, feeling like an idiot while Eric washed him, soaking his shorts and looking scared as hell. He felt like shit. Truthfully, he felt like crying. His mood turned black so fast, there was no stopping it. "I'm sorry."

Eric's gaze shot to his face. "Why are you sorry?"

Defeat fell heavily on Oakley's shoulders. "For making you take care of me. You shouldn't have to be doing this. I can do it myself."

A bright smile lit Eric's face. "This is my job, remember? It's what I signed on for when we got married. Plus, it's not like I mind getting to touch your sexy body."

Oakley wanted to feel better. He really did, but he didn't want this for Eric. Oakley hadn't expected things to go downhill this rapidly.

At his silence, Eric's smile slipped away. "Seriously, Oakley. I love you. You could've been really hurt. I'm surprised you didn't hit your head on the way down. You're all I have. So let me take care of you for my peace of mind."

With his back teeth locked, Oakley gave him a sharp nod. Fuck. This was a mess. He was all Eric had. Why had Oakley been so stupid? He hadn't thought this through. All Oakley had cared about was making his dream come true for a little while before he lost his chance. Now he had trapped Eric with him, because he knew damn well Eric wouldn't leave him. He was a bastard. Eric deserved so much better than him.

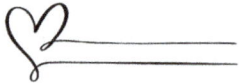

It took everything Eric possessed not to demand Oakley be real with him. This was worse than he realized. His insides shook. He hadn't been talking shit. Oakley could have been seriously hurt. If he had hit his head on the way down, he could have died. A huge bruise was already forming on his chest. Eric felt sick. If Oakley would just tell him the truth, they could create a care plan together. They could put some safety bars in the bathroom. Eric could start showering with him. This silence was stupid, but he couldn't force Oakley. Well, he could, but

Eric was scared as hell of Oakley's reaction. Oakley had more pride than anyone he had ever met. It was maddening.

Eric peeled off his wet clothes and tossed them in the hamper before drying Oakley's skin. Oakley let it happen, but he didn't look happy about it. Eric had to fix this and somehow save Oakley's pride. He wrapped the thick towel around Oakley, trapping his arms inside. Eric shuffled close and stole a kiss.

"I have you now, my little burrito." He brushed his lips across Oakley's again. "There's no escape." He moved toward the bedroom, herding Oakley toward the bed.

Oakley smiled at Eric's ridiculousness. "Oh no. What will you do with me?"

A wicked smile tugged at Eric's lips as he got Oakley settled on the bed and followed him down. "The same thing I do with every burrito I run across. Eat you." He playfully gnawed at Oakley's skin while keeping his weight off him. Oakley squirmed and laughed beneath him. Eric smiled against his skin.

"I love you so much."

Eric's eyes fell closed at Oakley's confession. He savored the words. "I love you too and don't you ever forget it." He rolled to his side and tucked Oakley against him. Eric didn't know how to coax him into being honest. He just wanted to talk this through. Eric needed Oakley to understand he could tell him anything and count on him. "I fell getting out of the shower at my aunt's place not long before we got married. I hit my elbow on the counter and slid like two feet." Eric chuckled. "Thought I'd taken my dick off and ended up with one hell of a knot on my arm. The older I get, the more it hurts to fall. In fact, I just stayed down for a few minutes to assess." Eric couldn't stop smiling because he felt stupid. Everyone did when they did something humiliating, even when no one saw.

Oakley chuckled. "Yeah. If you hadn't come in and pulled me off the floor, I probably would have chosen to stay down for a minute. It looks like I'll have some bruises to explain at my doctor's appointment tomorrow."

"You have a doctor's appointment tomorrow? Would you like me to come with you?"

Oakley never stopped smiling after his laugh. "Nah. It's just a six-month follow-up."

Goddamn it. He didn't know how much longer he could stay silent. "All right. Do you want to finish our movie, or are you ready to get some sleep?"

"I vote we make out."

Eric laughed, but he let himself get pulled into a kiss. Despite the secrets, Eric was still happier than he could recall ever being. He would take Oakley's half-truths over anything else in the world. When Eric fell, he always fell hard. In fact, some might say he was a little bit psycho. He had acted crazy as hell, trying to keep Jakk. Eric couldn't imagine how far he would go for the man who had unabashedly married him as quickly as possible. He would do anything. Honestly, he was a little terrified of himself.

Chapter Eight

NOW THAT ERIC KNEW the truth, it was a tad aggravating to realize how blind he had been. But Oakley was also damn good at casually doing things while keeping Eric distracted. As he watched Oakley down a handful of prescription pills, it occurred to him that he watched Oakley do this every day without thinking. Oakley would joke and talk while quickly getting what he needed. He would toss them back like nothing happened. Then he would turn the spinning rack in the kitchen cabinet, so it showed the spices rather than all his pill bottles. He was truly masterful in his act. Unfortunately, Eric knew the truth now and he couldn't stop noticing every single way Oakley kept his condition hidden from him.

Oakley set his water glass in the sink. "I shouldn't be gone more than two hours. When I get back, I was thinking of hitting the batting cages. Would you like to join me?"

"Of course." Eric fought to keep his cool. He honestly hoped Oakley didn't think he was an idiot. The guy certainly treated him like one. "I need to run down to that little corner market and stock up on some things. Our fridge is starting to look a little bare."

"Bodega," Oakley corrected.

Eric rolled his eyes. His smile turned genuine. "You New Yorkers and your goddamn bodegas."

Oakley chuckled as he moved to where Eric sat at the kitchen table. He swiped a kiss across Eric's lips. "I'll hurry back."

At the mention of hurrying, a lump formed in Eric's throat. Oakley could fall again, and Eric wouldn't be there. "Are you absolutely sure you don't want me to go?"

Oakley stole a deeper kiss. "Go do your shopping. You won't even notice I'm gone."

That wasn't true at all, but—as always—Eric couldn't force anything. "Okay. I hope everything goes okay."

Oakley flashed him a smile before heading for the door. "I love you."

"I love you too." Eric wasn't sure Oakley had even heard before he disappeared.

With defeat making his legs heavy, Eric grabbed the rolling cart and made his way to the store. He hadn't been far behind

Oakley, but he was nowhere to be seen. Eric prayed that meant he snagged a cab. As he walked inside, the tiny old lady who was always there called out her hellos. Eric hadn't lived with Oakley long before Hana had dragged every ounce of details about his life with Oakley from him. It seemed she knew everyone's business and Oakley had lived there a while. Eric was a new fact for her to add to his story.

The store was dead, so Hana did what she always did when they were slow, and he was there. She followed him around to talk. "How is that handsome husband? He should pay someone to do this for you."

An uncomfortable laugh escaped Eric. "He's good and I don't mind. I wouldn't get to come see you if he paid someone to shop for us."

"Awww. You're too sweet. It's just that if I had the money, I would be on a yacht somewhere or on a beach. Instead, he always stays here. It makes no sense."

"He loves New York." Eric grabbed a gallon of milk and some cheese.

"What about you? You don't miss your family back in California? You don't miss the weather?"

Eric shrugged. "Sometimes I miss the weather." He wouldn't talk about his family. "But I love Oakley more than I love the year-round warmth." Eric headed for the register with Hana in tow.

"You really are too sweet. I like you much better than Oakley's last husband."

Everything inside Eric froze. His brain refused to work.

Hana scanned his groceries with zero care for the destruction she caused. "That one used to strut in here with different men all the time. Just flaunting his cheating. I always wanted to tell Oakley, but Oakley always came in here with bruises. He would say it was baseball stuff, but I had an abusive husband once too. I know what getting punched in the face looks like." Hana shook her head. "I was too scared that rotten one would kill Oakley if I told him about the other men. Plus, I didn't know if maybe he knew, and they had an agreement. I didn't want to seem nosey or anything."

Eric would have laughed his ass off at that one if he could fucking breathe. The secrets just kept piling up. What else didn't he know? Oakley had kept a whole-ass first husband from him. Hell, maybe it wasn't even his first. Eric could be the third or fourth for all he knew.

Eric quickly paid for his groceries and made his way home. His mind reeled. It was not like Eric hadn't searched Oakley's name online. Surely the entire world would have known if Oakley had been married before. Then again, Jakk had kept Eric a secret for years. Eric was a complete mess. He blindly put away the food. Eric wouldn't be surprised later if he found milk in the cleaning closet. He simply ran on autopilot. His feet carried him through the large, upscale apartment. All this had belonged to another man once. Were there signs he had missed on that one too? Eric eyed every photo he passed. There was nothing. He wanted to tear the place apart and search every document he found. Eric really wanted to scream at the top of his lungs. It wasn't about the marriage. Yeah, that bothered him a little. Eric had loved the idea of being the guy who finally caught Oakley. But the fucking secrets. The lies by omission. How could a fresh marriage survive on half-truths? How much more of Oakley's silence could Eric endure before he broke? He very much feared he was already there. Eric felt sick.

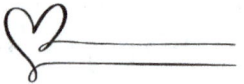

Oakley didn't feel better today. He had suggested the batting cages, hoping the exercise would loosen up his muscles. If nothing else, he hoped hitting some balls would distract him. He couldn't get home to Eric fast enough... and a pain pill. Seriously, he was dying.

Last night's bullshit made Oakley rethink a few things. First off, as much as he loved this city, it maybe wasn't the best place for him anymore. It wasn't easy to navigate in his condition and things would only get worse. That acceptance led to another.

Eric and he had promised their lives to each other. Oakley took that seriously. It seemed Eric did too. So Oakley had spent part of his appointment discussing moving his care plan to a doctor in California near Eric's mom. For better or worse, they were forever, and Oakley needed to be realistic. He needed a wheelchair-friendly home and a simpler town. That also meant—eventually—he would have to tell Eric everything.

The apartment was quiet when Oakley came through the door. He thought Eric was still out until he found him sitting at the table where he had left him.

Oakley put away his bag of prescriptions while eyeing Eric. "Is everything okay?" Eric didn't look like Eric. The way his eyes burned was a little scary.

"How was your appointment?"

Oakley shrugged. He knew he needed to come clean. This didn't feel like the right time. There was obviously something bothering Eric. "It was an appointment. Seriously, what's wrong?"

Eric's eyes filled with tears. He looked away and cleared his throat. "I keep hoping you'll eventually just tell the truth, but maybe you don't know what that is any longer."

Oh, fuck. That didn't sound good. Despite his best efforts, a nervous chuckle escaped him. "What do you mean?" He didn't want to assume anything.

Eric swiped at his eyes and met Oakley's stare. "I don't even know where to start with that question. Should we talk about the MS or your first husband first? Was he your first? I mean, it's not like I know you at all. He could've been your fifth for all I know."

Despite his horror and absolute confusion, Oakley's knees weakened. He grabbed the edge of the counter to stay upright. Eric shot to his feet, making matters worse. In a moment when Eric should let him fall, he still didn't.

He helped Oakley to the table. Oakley sat hard and winced. "Maybe let me take a pain pill before we fight."

A muscle worked in Eric's jaw, but he opened the cabinet and spun the spice rack. He looked at each bottle before finding the pain meds. After fixing him a glass of water and passing him a pill, Eric reclaimed his seat. All was done in complete silence. Oakley didn't know if he should scream or cry. Instead, he took his pill and took a breath.

"You're my first husband, so I'm confused as fuck by that one."

Eric didn't soften. "You're telling me Hana lied about hating the husband before me who always cheated and beat you? Did she imagine all that, or are you saying she's the consummate liar of you two?"

Oakley flinched. He supposed he deserved that. "Oh."

"Oh?" Eric sounded truly terrifyingly angry now.

Oakley rushed to fix it. "I swear, you're my first husband. There was a guy who lived here with me for a couple of years, but we were never married."

"You never said anything."

A bitter smile tugged at Oakley's lips. "Some things are better left in the past and I would never disrespect you by talking about my exes. Plus, he's a piece of shit. I don't like remembering him."

Eric swiped his hand across his eyes before focusing on him again. "I feel like I married a complete stranger. You don't tell me anything. I had to stand there today and act like I already knew everything Hana said. Just like I had to sit there at the charity game and pretend I knew you have MS while Rocky praised me for not being scared to marry you in spite of your illness."

Goddamn. It was worse than he thought. Eric had known for weeks. He had known through every wince and his fall. Oakley looked like the liar Eric accused him of being. "I'm sorry."

"You're sorry? You made me feel like a fucking fool."

Oakley took a steadying breath. He really hurt today, and Eric deserved better. Panic hit from nowhere. Maybe he didn't want this life anymore. "Maybe I'm done." Once the hysteria left his lips, it was over. Oakley couldn't catch his breath or pull back. Truthfully, he hadn't allowed himself to process the news fully yet. He had been in a bit of a daze about his situation, unable to cope with the shock. Eric's fury made everything so very real and hopeless. "I swear I wasn't trying to trick you into marrying a cripple. That was never my intention. I just fell so hard in love with you, I was scared as hell to miss my chance. Then things got worse so much faster than I expected. But I fully realize you don't deserve to be stuck with me. So maybe I'm done. If I'm gone, you'll get everything and you'll be free. You can find someone who deserves you—"

Eric slapped his hand down on the table so fast and hard, Oakley jumped. "Would everyone please stop fucking saying that to me?" Eric screamed the words, as if beyond conversation. "I choose who's worthy of me.

I choose who deserves my time. Goddamn. Do you have any idea how fucking hurtful those words are? How condescending? Find someone who deserves you," Eric mocked. "I fucking know what I'm worth. That's just a goddamn excuse to break me. And if you think for one fucking second you're going to die on me, you're a goddamn idiot." He had never seen Eric enraged. It was kind of hot and snapped Oakley from his panic attack. Unfortunately, though, Eric wasn't done. "In fact, if you ever even say that to me again, I'll call the police and have you put on a psych hold. I swear to God I will. Just try me. I won't be manipulated like that."

"I would never try to manipulate you."

Eric slapped the table again. "Did I say I was fucking finished? You will tell me everything and I mean everything from here on out. I will be going to these appointments and how fucking dare you doubt me? Do you think I'm shallow? Do you think I'm weak? Do you think my love is so flimsy, it would collapse under a treatable disease? Any disease, for that matter." He stared at Oakley, barely blinking. "Well?"

"I didn't know if I was allowed to talk yet," Oakley admitted.

Eric growled.

Oakley made a calming gesture. "None of those things kept me silent. I just…" Oakley's hands rose and fell. "You've been through so much, and I wanted to be your happiness and peace." He took a deep breath. Oakley knew he could tell Eric anything, especially things he couldn't tell anyone else. "And I'm wrecked." His voice broke. Oakley cleared his throat. "Absolutely shattered, actually. I'm being told I'm no longer the person who made it all the way to more than a decade of pro. That guy is gone. It's not like I thought I'd go back to pro or some shit. I just didn't expect I would lose everything about myself after retirement. How do I go from being the guy who constantly stays active to being told to sit down? I'm trying like hell to figure it out. I guess I didn't know what to say to you. You didn't fall in love with a disabled man. I didn't know what to say," Oakley repeated. It honestly came down to that. He didn't know how to explain what he didn't know. Oakley didn't know what his future looked like. So how could he reassure Eric about their life together?

"I fell in love with your heart." Eric's soul was in his eyes. "All those nights on the phone when you didn't let me feel alone. All those times you were proud to be seen with me when no one else ever had been. You can't know how you stole me. I would rather be with you under any circumstances than anyone else in the world, but I can't make you see that. I can't make you see me."

The urge to cry was massive. His voice gave that secret away. "I knew you'd stay. That's what makes me the bad guy. I saw you, fell in love, and stayed silent, all while knowing you would stay. What does that tell you about me?" He already knew. Oakley knew he was selfish.

A sweet smile touched Eric's lips. "It tells me you're as scared of losing me as I am you."

So much hit Oakley at once. Too much. He tried to speak, but his voice only sounded like a hoarse whisper. "I don't want to do this alone."

Eric leaned forward and took his hand. His gaze never wavered from holding Oakley's stare. "You're not alone. That's not because you trapped me. It's because I love you and we're in this life together."

He meant it. Oakley had no idea why this amazing man chose him, but he had. "I really need some help today." That admission took everything Oakley had, but he was tired, and he hurt. Life felt like moving through quicksand and he was drowning.

With a nod, Eric stood. He helped Oakley to his feet. "Come on. Lean on me."

Oakley knew he gave Eric too much of his weight, but Eric didn't complain. He helped Oakley to bed. While Oakley sat on the edge of their mattress, Eric undressed him like he would a child. Oakley might have been humiliated, but it was Eric.

Eric winced at the ugly bruises from last night's fall. "Damn, baby. What can I do?"

Oakley answered as Eric tucked him in. "Will you hold me?"

Eric circled the bed. "I'd already planned to do that. Do you need anything else?"

Oakley shook his head. "Just your love."

Eric's eyes burned with intensity when he met Oakley's stare. "You have that."

He knew. Goddamn. It was amazing and beautiful. Eric stripped down to his underwear and then molded against Oakley. Oakley sighed in relief. There was no scientific reason for him to feel better for being in Eric's arms, but he did. So much tension eased from him. He understood they still had so much left to talk about, and they would. For now, though, Oakley needed a nap. He needed Eric.

Chapter Nine

A NAP CLEARED ERIC'S head. It helped that Oakley was in his arms. Eric kept placing light kisses on his hair, trying not to wake him, but he couldn't stop. His heart demanded his affection go somewhere. Oakley's expression as he had confessed everything haunted Eric. The pain and suffering Oakley had hidden from him was way more than Eric anticipated. It broke his heart. Eric had been right here, more than willing to be the rock. He hated Oakley hadn't trusted more in their relationship. Fast marriage or not, they were strong. They were meant to be. Oakley would never fight alone.

He couldn't stand to see the dark bruises Oakley sported. Eric knew they probably were only a tiny fraction of the pain Eric couldn't see. He wanted to make it better. Eric just didn't know how to help, so he let Oakley sleep.

Oakley's cellphone rang on the bedside table. Before Eric could silence it, Oakley's arm shot out. He blindly patted the table until he found the device. Oakley answered and switched the call to speaker.

"Hello?" There was no missing the grogginess in Oakley's voice.

"Did I wake you?"

Eric didn't recognize the voice.

"Yeah, but it's cool. What's up?"

"A bunch of us have thrown together a softball game at the park. Are you in?"

Oakley scrubbed his face. "Yeah. What time?"

Eric shot him a death glare. He couldn't believe Oakley planned to play ball feeling like this.

Oakley made a calming gesture.

"We're meeting in two hours. If your man is coming, tell him to bring a chair. You know how it is. It's literally just us throwing down some bases in the grass."

"Yeah. I'll make sure we bring everything."

"Cool. See you then."

The call disconnected and Eric tried hard not to lose his shit. "You're on the edge of death today and you want to play ball?"

Oakley smiled. It was one of his big, goofy ones Eric couldn't resist.

Eric wanted to punch him.

"Baby. My doctor has advised me to stay as active as possible. Exercise helps with maintaining balance, range of motion, and energy levels. Plus, it keeps the depression at bay. I'm not ready to give up yet. Okay?"

Fuck. He hated Oakley sounded reasonable. He didn't want his panic and worry to be the thing that made Oakley worse. Eric knew nothing about Oakley's instructions from his doctor, since he never told him anything. At least he was invited. Eric could watch over him.

"Okay. I trust you."

Oakley laughed. "Don't sound so disappointed about it."

Now Eric felt guilty. "I'm not. I'm just—"

"Adjusting to a new reality," Oakley finished for him. "I know. Me too. But I'm not ready to give up yet, so please don't stop believing in me, okay?"

"Never." Eric kissed his forehead. "I guess we should get up and moving if we plan to go to the park." He paused as a thought hit. "Whoever that was didn't say which park."

Oakley chuckled. "Don't worry. I know which park Adley meant. We always go to the same one. He's an old teammate," Oakley clarified.

Eric nodded. "I remember meeting him at the wedding."

Oakley rolled to his side. He draped his leg over Eric's hip and scooted closer. "We don't have to get up yet."

Eric's body immediately responded. "Are you teasing me?"

An evil-looking smile stretched Oakley's lips. "Have I ever teased you?"

Eric couldn't think with Oakley looking at him like that. "I don't know. I'll think about it later."

With a shove, Eric was on his back, with Oakley straddling him. Eric sucked in a breath when Oakley rolled his hips, creating fiction between their cocks. Oakley did it again as he buried his face against the crook of Eric's neck. He sucked as he rocked against Eric.

Eric groaned. "This would be so much better without underwear between us."

A wicked chuckle rumbled against Eric's skin. Oakley kept moving against him, refusing to give him more. Eric stayed still and took it because he was too enthralled to move. His breathing turned ragged despite the clothes between them. It was obvious

Oakley fully intended to make Eric come in his underwear. He refused to be alone. Eric grabbed Oakley's hips and lifted, doing his best to drive Oakley crazy. Oakley made a sound that drove Eric to go harder. He used his strength to move Oakley exactly the way he wanted.

Oakley began to pant.

Eric had no mercy.

When Oakley cried out against Eric's skin, it sent Eric spinning. He gasped and moaned his way through the ecstasy. Eric hadn't come in his clothes since he was a teen. Life with Oakley was always unexpected.

"I love you."

Oakley whispered the words against the shell of Eric's ear. Eric's eyes unexpectedly filled with tears. It had been such a rollercoaster day, and he was the happiest he had ever been. Sometimes Eric didn't know where to go with that. He had never been this scared to lose.

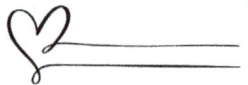

While he waited on his turn to bat, Chipper eyed the nymph on the sidelines—deep in conversation with Eric. Goddamn. He was adorable. Chipper could put the guy in his pocket. They had crossed paths a few times. All Chipper knew was Baylor was a highly sought after wedding planner and he seemed to hate Chipper for some odd reason. This was new territory for Chipper. Everyone liked him. But every time Chipper tried to approach Baylor, the guy ran. At first, it had been cute. Baylor was all put together and adorable. Chipper just thought he made the guy nervous. Now he wasn't as sure that was the reason, and Chipper was obsessed.

"Why do you keep watching Eric and Baylor? You only look this intense when you're in the cage. While I'm a thousand percent sure you can take me, I'll definitely try holding my own if you're about to attack my husband."

Chipper tried rearranging his features at Oakley's lecture. He realized how harsh he probably looked. "Sorry. No. It's Baylor. Why doesn't the guy like me? I haven't done shit to him."

Oakley snorted. "Dude, you hit on the guy like he's a cheap whore every time you cross paths with him. Maybe you should try talking to him like a normal person." Oakley brightened. "From what I understand, he handles more than weddings. You should try to hire him to put together something for you."

"Like what?" Even Chipper heard the annoyance in his voice. He didn't like being interested in someone who made him work.

Oakley shrugged. "I don't know. When's your next big fight? You could have him plan your victory celebration, or your mom's birthday. Use your imagination."

"When is your man's next birthday? We could plan him a huge surprise party."

Oakley shook his head. "For such a talented fighter, you're looking very chicken shit right now, but fine. If you need me to help, I'm in."

A huge grin split Chipper's face. "Since you're helping, I'll let the chicken shit comment slide."

Without waiting to learn any details about Eric's birthday, Chipper let out a loud whistle. "Yo, Baylor."

Baylor's entire body stiffened. A sexy and annoyed looking green gaze swung his way. Damn. He would be fire in bed. "Wait for me after the game. It's business related."

Baylor gave him a sharp nod and went back to talking to Eric.

A wicked chuckle rumbled under Chipper's breath. He had the guy now. Baylor just didn't know it yet.

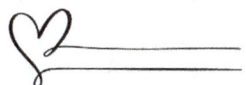

Nothing had changed really, but Oakley felt differently about life today. He was still headed down the same difficult path, but he knew he wasn't alone anymore. What had once felt unbearable and insurmountable now looked a little less bleak. That was Eric and his beautiful heart. Oakley was well aware he didn't deserve him. He wouldn't change a damn thing about them.

Chipper's suggestion about a party for Eric had started—in Oakley's mind—as just helping himself while helping a friend. As the game had gone on, the idea grew. Eric deserved to be celebrated. He deserved everything. Oakley grabbed his phone from his ball bag and shot off an email and a few texts. He would make sure Eric got the whole world. Oakley would start the moment he finished this game.

After saying a bunch of goodbyes, Oakley slung the bag over one shoulder and Eric's collapsible camping chair over the other.

Eric huffed. "Let me carry those."

"No." Oakley chuckled at Eric's irritation as he walked away.

Giving up, Eric fell into step beside him. "Did you have fun?"

"I need the exercise and it's always good to see the guys."

Oakley fell back a hair. He wrapped his arms around Eric and walked in step with him to the apartment. Eric laughed at his playfulness but didn't try to get away. Oakley kissed his ear.

"I love you."

He saw Eric's cheek curve with a smile. "I love you too."

"Thank you for coming today. I liked having you there. You seemed to enjoy your time with Baylor."

Eric glanced over his shoulder. "I like watching you play. As for Baylor, it seems he's in town because he's best friends with someone named Bandit. So he got dragged along, but he's actually really nice. I thought he was kind of stiff when he planned our wedding. He was a lot more laid back today."

Oakley decided to give Eric a little breathing room and took his hand instead. "Yeah. I've never been sure if Bandit's real name is Bandit, but he's that red-haired guy who plays soccer for New England."

Eric nodded. "That makes sense. Baylor said he was actually from Vermont, but he's done so many celebrity weddings from simply word of mouth that he doesn't even have a permanent residence any longer. He goes where the money is, and then crashes with Bandit when he has time off. Apparently, they went to high school together."

"The guy is seriously wrecking Chipper's ego." Oakley threw the words out there in case Eric had gotten any insight.

Eric laughed. "I think Chipper could use a little humbling."

That was true. "Meh. I'm sure the same has been said of me at some point."

"And how does that make you feel?" Eric asked in his most professional voice, making Oakley laugh.

"I don't give a fuck. Cockiness won me the most amazing husband in the world, and a fuck ton of baseball games, but those are nowhere near as important."

Eric's smile never dimmed. "I suppose it was pretty bold of you to dump a drink in my lap."

"Did I ever apologize for that? Legitimately, I mean."

Eric didn't respond until after the doorman opened the door to their apartment building for them. "Are you sorry?"

Oakley reached past him and hit the button to call the elevator. "Not really, no. You never would have looked my way without that drink."

As the elevator carried them to their floor, Eric leaned his shoulder against the wall and held Oakley's stare. "Oh. I don't know. We're pretty damn meant to be. I think we would've found each other no matter what."

Before Oakley could respond, his phone chirped. He dug it out and checked his messages. Seeing what he had been waiting for, Oakley opened his emails and found the one he just got. He passed the phone to Eric. "Pick out our new house in California."

Eric froze with his fingers wrapped around Oakley's phone. He didn't take it. "What do you mean?"

A grin stretched Oakley's lips. He loved getting the drop on Eric. Oakley wanted to give him everything, especially happiness. "Your mom is in California, so are a bunch of top MS specialists. I don't know when, but eventually, this city will be too hard for me to navigate. So, pick out our house." He made Eric take the phone. "I texted a realtor friend of mine and asked her to send me a list of places that are close to your mom, the doctors I need, and not too far from the beach. Choose."

Eric didn't look at the phone. He stared at Oakley in disbelief. "We're moving to California?"

The doors slid open, freeing them from the elevator. Oakley shuffled Eric into their apartment. "Come on. Sit down. Let's see our choices."

"You're really being serious."

Oakley didn't know what Eric had a hard time grasping. "Why are you this shocked?

You know I love you. You heard my reasoning."

Eric didn't respond until they were settled on the couch. "Because I was more than ready to live out my life with you here, and I know how much you love New York."

He held Eric's stare. "I found something I love more."

Eric truly looked ready to cry.

Oakley took the phone from him and cuddled close, forcing Eric to hold him. "Come on. Let's pick a few choices together. We can let Khloe know and fly out tomorrow to look at them." Rather than wait for Eric to complain some more, he started clicking links. It didn't take long for Eric to get into the spirit and give his input. Oakley was oddly excited to open a new chapter in his life. He couldn't wait to give Eric a better life than he had ever known.

Chapter Ten

IT WAS SOMEWHAT STRANGE to be back, living in California again. He tried to stay out of the movers' way while still pointing out where everything went. The travel and stress had worn on Oakley. Eric had made sure the bedroom was done first and sent Oakley to bed.

"Knock. Knock."

Eric glanced toward the door.

Chipper stood in the doorway, smiling like an idiot. "Your door was open. I came by with a housewarming gift."

Eric accepted the present Chipper held. He didn't open it. Eric was too stunned to see the guy. "Where in the hell do you actually live? You turn up everywhere."

A soft laugh rumbled from Chipper. "I don't like to sit still, but I actually live here. Not here, here, but about forty miles south of here. Originally, I'm from Nevada, but I moved to California some years back to train with the best: Maverick Kapra."

When Eric stared at him with zero recognition, Chipper expounded. "He's won heavyweight champion like a gazillion times."

"Oh." Eric didn't follow MMA. "That sounds amazing. Thank you for this, by the way," he said, motioning toward the box he held.

"You're welcome. It's a personalized cheese board. This is a nice place." He turned in a circle, eyeing everything.

Eric laughed. "Damn. You didn't even give me time to open it."

Chipper's smiling face turned his way. His light brown eyes were incredibly sweet. Despite hitting people for a living, Chipper always seemed like a kind soul. "Sorry. I don't like surprises. They're rarely pleasant. Where's Oakley hiding?"

Eric turned away so Chipper couldn't read his expression. He set the box on the coffee table. "The move has been exhausting. I asked him to rest." Eric didn't know who all knew about Oakley's illness. He didn't want to say anything that might upset Oakley.

Chipper made a humming sound, bringing Eric's gaze back his way. Again, Chipper eyed the house. Eric studied him, trying to read him. The guy had a jaw that could cut glass and a body that would make anyone drool. Eric wasn't sure why Baylor didn't jump at the chance to enjoy him.

Suddenly, Chipper focused on him. "You're a good person. I'm glad Oakley found you."

Eric fought not to blush. He wasn't good with such direct praise. "Thank you, but I'm the lucky one. He showed up in my life exactly when I needed to be saved and loved me when I thought no one ever would again." Eric had no idea why he admitted such a thing. Chipper just had a way of looking at people—like he saw them. It tricked the mind into believing they were closer friends than they were.

"You just described him exactly how he describes you."

Eric wanted to melt. Every day, Eric discovered again exactly how blessed he was. Sometimes it was overwhelming, but always amazing. "Would you like a tour?"

Chipper brightened. "Sounds great. I love the neighborhood. Maybe I can move in next door, and we could have cookouts and shit."

It hit Eric. Everything about Chipper suddenly made sense. The nonstop travel, the popping up everywhere, and even the intense way he chased Baylor looked completely clear now. Chipper was lonely. Eric knew then he would do whatever he could to set him up with Baylor. Chipper was a good man. He deserved to know the same happiness Eric lived every day. Eric wanted everyone to feel like this. He prayed it never stopped.

The bed dipped next to Oakley. Eric crawled into his arms. Oakley smiled as their bodies molded. God, he was just so sickeningly in love. Oakley would have thought things would have cooled at least a little by now, but no. Every day, this feeling grew bigger. They grew stronger.

"Are the movers already gone?"

Eric kissed his chest. "Already? You've been asleep for five hours."

Oakley blinked. Damn. He must have been more tired than he realized. Luckily, he had Eric to watch out for him and send him to bed when he needed the push to rest. "Wow. I didn't realize."

He felt Eric shrug. "You were doing what your body needed. Chipper stopped by," Eric added before Oakley could quip about doing Eric being what his body needed. "He brought us a personalized cheese board."

Oakley took a second to fully wake before responding. "That was nice of him. I guess he must be home for once."

"Does he know?"

Oakley could have pretended not to know what Eric meant, but he wouldn't do that. He understood Eric's position. Eric needed to hear he wasn't the last to know. That was one thing he could give him. "Yeah. He knows, but I only recently told him. I didn't decide to start telling my friends until after you knew. Not only did I think you should know first—other than Rocky, since he books my jobs—but I also don't think I'm ready for it to hit the media."

Eric stroked his stomach before shoving his hand beneath Oakley's shirt so he could rub bare skin. "You don't have to explain. I just wasn't sure how much to say when he asked where you were. I want you in control of your business."

Oakley never stopped being blown away by Eric's thoughtfulness. "Thanks for that. I still haven't told many people, but my closest friends know now. You're probably exhausted. Why don't you close your eyes for a little while? I'll hold you."

He swore he felt Eric's smile. "I think we'll have a really nice life here."

Oakley snorted. "Nice? No. We'll have a fucking phenomenal life here. It's us. We're together. How could it be any other way?"

"That's true." Eric kissed his chest again and snuggled even closer, as if settling in. "It'll be the greatest life of all."

Oakley smiled at the way Eric's voice drifted as he obviously dozed off. Sometimes, it hit him again out of nowhere. He held his best friend. Eric let him love him. Oakley had been at a point of bleakness no one could understand, before Eric had looked at him, all annoyed at Oakley's accusation of stalking, and caught him, saving him from the spiral. That was the moment Oakley's entire future shifted from hopeless to beautiful. Oakley would never let Eric forget how loved he was. For whatever time Oakley had left on this earth, he would make Eric smile. He listened to Eric breathe and knew fate always had a plan. It was better than he could have ever dreamed.

Keep an eye out for the next Sporting Pride, *Fighting Fate*.

Please consider leaving a review at the retailer where you purchased this book. Reviews really help with a book's visibility, which allows me to continue writing more stories. Thank you, Charity.

About the Author

CHARITY PARKERSON IS AN award-winning and multi-published author with several companies. Born with no filter from her brain to her mouth, she decided to take this odd quirk and insert it in her characters. One of her greatest loves is writing morally gray characters. You'll find them scattered throughout her hundreds of titles.

*Eight-time Readers' Favorite Award Winner

*2015 Passionate Plume Award Finalist

*2013 Reviewers' Choice Award Winner

*2012 ARRA Finalist for Favorite Paranormal Romance

*Five-time winner of The Mistress of the Darkpath

Connect with her online:

*Sign up for her newsletter: https://bit.ly/charityparkersonnewsletter

*Join her readers' group on Facebook: http://bit.ly/CharitysTribe

* Website: https://www.charityparkerson.com

*A list of her social media accounts and giveaways all in one place: http://hy.page/charityparkerson

www.ingramcontent.com/pod-product-compliance
Lightning Source LLC
Chambersburg PA
CBHW070936250626
47159CB00009B/3278